MONA the VAMPIRE

The Hairy Hands

CINAR

Television series © 1999 Fancy Cape Productions Inc.
a subsidiary of CINAR Corporation/Alphanim, France
3, Canal J. All rights reserved.

ORCHARD BOOKS
96 Leonard Street, London EC2A 4XD
Orchard Books Australia
14 Mars Road, Lane Cove, NSW 2066
First published in Great Britain in 1996
This edition published in 2000
ISBN 1-84121-859-6
Text © Hiawyn Oram
Illustrations © Sonia Holleyman
The right of Hiawyn Oram to be identified as the
Author and Sonia Holleyman as the Illustrator of this
Work has been asserted by them in accordance with
the Copyright, Designs and Patents Act, 1988.
A CIP catalogue record for this book is available from
the British Library.
1 3 5 7 9 10 8 6 4 2
Printed in the United Kingdom

MONA the VAMPIRE

The Hairy Hands

Hiawyn Oram

Illustrated by
Sonia Holleyman

 ORCHARD BOOKS

Contents

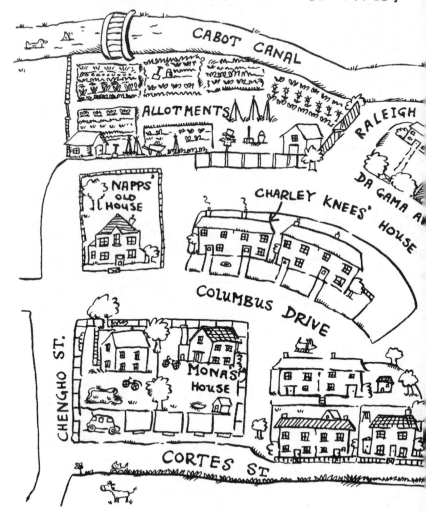

COLUMBUS CLOSE off OLD STREET

CABOT CANAL

ALLOTMENTS

RALEIGH

DA GAMA A

3 NAPPS' OLD HOUSE

CHARLEY KNEES' HOUSE

COLUMBUS DRIVE

CHENGHO ST.

MONAS' HOUSE

CORTES ST.

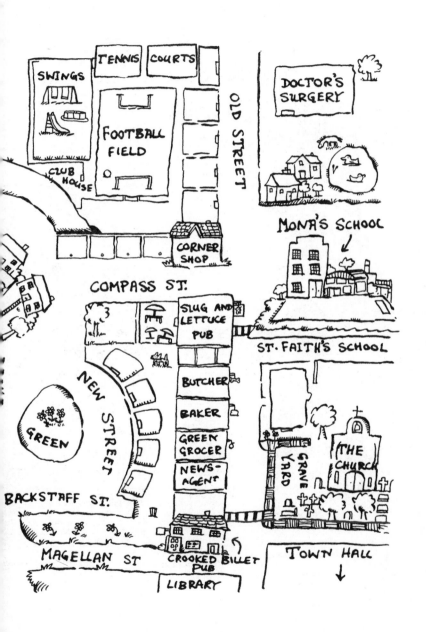

The Cast

Mona

Fang

Charley-Knees

Lily
(Second Vampire)

Hairy Hands

Mum

Mr Bones

Chapter 1
Stuntmen Never Cry

Mona's mother and Lily's mother were in the kitchen making their own medicines with herbs from their own gardens. When the fog and the peppermint fumes got too much, Mona, Lily and Fang went out to ride their bikes with Charley-Knees.

Charley-Knees lived opposite. His real name was Charley Bones. Everyone just called him Charley-Knees because of his nobbly knees.

Mona, however, never noticed his knees. Only his nature. For Charley was the boy in Mona's class who loved danger. And Charley was the boy in Mona's class who never cried.

"You must have ONE time," said Lily, as they pedalled round Columbus Drive. "One time when you hurt yourself <u>so</u> bad it really, really, REALLY hurt."

The Boy who never cried

11

"Nope," said Charley-Knees.

From Mona's saddlebag, Fang sat up and hissed.

Mona translated...

Fang says you're fibbing

"Then he's the one fibbing," said Charley-Knees, taking out a packet of crisps and opening it without stopping pedalling.

"I didn't even cry when I fell off the fridge and knocked my front teeth into my *skull*! I didn't even cry when George Jamell pushed me into a cactus plant and I had eight squillion cactus thorns stuck in me!"

"But *why*?" said Lily, who felt like crying just at the thought of eight squillion thorns stuck in her.

Charley screeched his bike to a halt and sauntered over to a piece of chipboard lying with some bricks near the hedge. "Because stuntmen don't cry. Whatever happens to them," he said, putting one end of the board on the bricks to make a ramp. "Not that you lot even know what a stuntman is. Do you?"

Mona, Lily and Fang shook their heads.

"Then watch this!" said Charley-Knees. Getting back on his bike, he pedalled off down the drive. When he was almost out of sight, he turned, stood up on his pedals and gave a blood-curdling whoop. Then, with head down over his handlebars, in a most blood-curdling way, he rode for the ramp.

Chapter 2
A Clear Case of the Hairy Hands

WHOOOSH!
GEREECH!
CON-GER-TI-NA-CRUNCH!

Charley and bike whizzed past, hit the board, shot over the hedge and disappeared into the Napps' old garden.

Fang's fur stood on end.

Lily sucked hard on a finger. "He's crashed," she whispered.

Mona threw down her bike. "Then we'd better see if he's all right!"

Slithering through a gap in the hedge, they raced across the uncut grass towards the scene of the crash. But before they'd even got to it, Mona could see something was wrong.

Charley's bike

Though Charley's bike was there, bent, buckled and with one wheel spinning, Charley wasn't. Not even a tuft of his hair or a shred of his jeans.

"Bbbbut. . . where is he?" stammered Lily.

Vanished sniggered Fang.

"How?" breathed Lily.

Mona stared round the deserted garden. She looked over at the house. As the Napps had moved out months ago, the windows were all tightly closed. Someone had hammered a piece of board over the glass in the back door.

No one could have got in. *Or could they?*

A zingy feeling started to buzz in Mona's head. A very zingy feeling that began quietly but soon grew to a loud certainty.

There was going to have to be something that could reach out and completely take away a boy of Charley's

size so quickly and all at once.

And that Thing, she decided in a flash, was the Hairy Hands.

Chapter 3
Lily Has Her Own Ideas

"Hairy Hands? What Hairy Hands?" screeched Lily as they ran for Mona's bedroom.

"They're like the troll in Billy Goats Gruff," said Mona, diving under the bed. "Except much bigger. And they just reach out and take anything they feel like. Even a whole car on a bridge."

"That's not true," said Lily.

"IT IS!" Mona wriggled out from under the bed clutching her box of vampire things. "But don't worry. Vampires can make Hairy Hands give back what they took. In fact vampires are the only thing that can."

"I bet parents could," said Lily. "Your mother could. With her karate. Or her peppermint potions."

"No," said Mona, giving Fang his wings and starting to draw circles round her eyes with red crayon. "Parents can't even see Hairy Hands. When Hairy Hands take their children, parents just say 'oh it was an accident,' or 'I told you if you did that you'd end up in that ditch.'. So you'd better get ready."

Lily sat down on Mona's bed. "I'd rather watch TV," she said.

"OK," said Mona. She had a new vampire cloak – one of the old dining room curtains – and she was busy seeing how well it would swirl. "But if you won't come with me to get back Charley-Knees I won't be your friend probably till Christmas."

Lily imagined not playing with Mona till Christmas – whenever that was – and it looked almost worse than being a vampire wrestling with a pair of Hairy Hands.

"All *right*," she sighed. "What can I have?"

"The spiders and my dressing gown for a cloak. And I'll make your front teeth black. . ." Mona waved a black crayon, "and you can twist your hair into frightening knots like me and just be the Second Vampire."

Lily sat down beside Mona, her face like a dark cloud. Then suddenly, she brightened.

"Maybe," she said, "the Hairy Hands are *friendly* Hairy Hands. Maybe they just took Charley-Knees to give him a holiday. In China or somewhere. With his grandmother."

In silence, Mona considered Lily's idea. As it happens she liked it. What she didn't like was Lily having it since she liked to be the one with all the good ideas.

Finally, she stood up, stuck in her glow-in-the-dark fangs, checked her scariness in the mirror and announced, "OK. Maybe they're friendly. Maybe they're not. But it's still only vampires they'll listen to. So come on. Let's go!"

Chapter 4
Through the Dog Flap

Mona the First Vampire, Lily the Second Vampire and Fang the Vampire Cat stood surveying the back of the Napps' old house.

"Nothing could've got in here," said Lily. "We can go home now."

"Don't be silly," said Mona. "Hairy Hands can move through walls. They're like dotted lines. They're like GHOSTS!"

"But Charley isn't," said Lily. "How could they get Charley in?"

Mona knelt down and pushed at something set in the bottom of the back door. It moved.

"Through here, of course," she said. "And so can we."

Never! hissed Fang.

"You'll do as I say," said Mona grabbing Fang and pushing him, hissing and spitting like a real vampire cat, through the flap.

Then she turned to Lily. "But not you, Second Vampire. You stand guard here. In case the Hairy Hands are still in the garden."

And without stopping to listen to Lily's wails of 'not by myself!' Mona wriggled as vampirishly as possible into whatever had to be done to save Charley-Knees.

Chapter 5
Two Shocks That Weren't Such Shocks

Immediately, she wished she hadn't. She'd been in the house when the Napps had lived in it and it had been nice and cosy. Now, empty of furniture and empty of Napps, it seemed huge and frightening.

She felt about the size of a mouse. Or even a mouse dropping. And there were plenty of those.

Fang had skitted off following their trail and was completely ignoring her furious whispers to return.

"Ho he," Mona sighed to herself. "It's scary being a vampire when there's no one to watch over you. Especially when you're really a little girl. So I'll just shout out to them and rush back and tell Lily they've gone out the chimney way."

HAIRY HANDS GIVE US CHARLEY-KNEES THIS INSTANT

But then she suddenly remembered
something. This wasn't just a game.
Charley-Knees *had* disappeared. And
probably only she knew why or how.

Taking a deep breath, she took out her
fangs, and stepped quietly into the hall.
On all fours and just as quietly, she
climbed the stairs. On the landing she
paused.

There was a sound coming from the front room. A sound that gave Mona a terrible shock that at the same time wasn't such a shock.

Holding her breath, she peered round the door. The room was empty except for some dusty board games and an old sofa across one corner.

Almost covering her frightening face with her cloak, she tiptoed over, knelt on the ragged seat and peeped over the back.

And that was when she got the second terrible shock that wasn't such a shock. Charley-Knees, the boy who never cried, was huddled there. And he was crying.

Chapter 6
Lily Goes For Help And Comes Back With Trouble

Charley stared at Mona. Mona stared at Charley. Mona opened her mouth to say, 'It's OK, Charley, when you crash your bike that hard that's a time you're supposed to cry.'.

Charley opened his mouth to say, 'This isn't crying just noises like crying.'.

But before either could speak there was an angry roar from downstairs.

"CHARLEEEEEE. YOU COME OUT OF THERE AT ONCE! D'YOU HEAR! OR I'LL KNOCK YOUR BLOCK OFF!"

Charley's red face paled.

"Don't worry," said Mona. "It wasn't you. It was the Hairy Hands. They took you in here *and* they did that to your bike."

"What?" said Charley, standing up shakily.

"The Hairy Hands," said Mona. "Big as anything and like ghosts and they just scoop up anything they want to.'"

"My Dad won't believe that," said Charley.

"Yes he will," said Mona, "if–"

She was interrupted by more banging of the dog flap and more yelling from Mr Bones about Charley getting a proper walloping if he didn't get down there at once.

Then Mona heard her own mother calling. "Mona! This is not funny. Come along out now."

"I know what's happened!" said Mona. "Lily got scared and ran and told them."

"We'd better go down," said Charley.

"No," said Mona. "Not you. Not for a walloping. And anyway then everyone'll see you cried. I'll go. I'll say the Hands have taken you out the chimney, back to their Headquarters in the allotments."

Mona ran to
the fireplace,
got some soot
and rubbed it
on Charley's face.

"There. Now all you have to do is sneak out the dog flap and go to the allotments by the short cut through the hedges. Then just look like you're picking peas or something for the Hairy Hands because you're their servant."

And, not waiting for Charley to argue, Mona put in her glow-in-the-darks and grabbed Fang – who'd given up on mice and was washing himself in a pool of sunlight.

At the door she turned. "By the way," she said, "the Hairy Hands are sort of half-friendly and only half not. So don't worry. They do give you back. In the end."

Chapter 7
Mona's Mother is Drawn In

"AAAAARGH!" Mona the Vampire's face appeared at the dog flap.

"Yaaaaaargh!" Mr. Bones jumped.

"Oh, *Mona*!" her mother cried. "You're impossible. Where's Charley?"

Mona pointed upwards. "There," she said solemnly.

"Where?" the mothers said, scanning the sky.

"WHERE?" growled Mr Bones glaring at Mona.

"There! Up there! The Hairy Hands' have got him. He's all right though. He's waving at us with his face all sooty from the chimney. *Can't you see?*"

Believing completely in what she was saying, Mona *could* see Charley, swinging his legs over the side of the Hairy Hands. Lily and the others could just about see him too. Only Mr Bones was disbelieving.

"Mrs Nashley!" he shouted. "Will you tell your kid to stop talking such–"

"And look! Look now!" Mona interrupted. She ran over to the hedge, away from the dog flap. "Now they're whooshing him to their Headquarters in the allotments. If we go down there, that's where he'll be. But we'd better hurry..."

Quick! Before they take him to China...

"Mona, please!" said Mona's mother as if Mona was going too far. "Lily's told us what happened."

Mona glared at Lily. "But she couldn't have," she said. "She wasn't looking when the Hands took Charley and crunched his bike. And she never went in the house so she never saw what Fang

and me saw which was the Hands playing … er … Shakes and Ladders … with Charley before they shooshed him out the chimney … didn't we Fang?"

Fang hissed that possibly, probably or even almost certainly they had seen exactly that.

"See?" said Mona.

"SEE?" exploded Mr Bones. "SEE?

You really expect me to stomach all this nonsense and then listen to a CAT? Charley's crashed his bike doing something stupid and now he's too afraid to own up." Still ranting, Mr Bones marched back to the dog flap to do some more yelling.

Knowing that at any moment he might meet Charley face to face, Mona decided there was no time to lose. She'd have to draw her mother in.

"Mum," she tugged at her mother's hand. Eyeing Mona suspiciously, her mother bent down.

"Please," Mona whispered in her best, most-pleading whisper, "make him believe me or Charley's going to get a terrible walloping. You said parents should never, ever do that to their kids whatever happens."

"Hmmm." Mona's mother gave a deep sigh. Then she walked quickly over to Mr Bones, and spoke to him in a way that none of them could hear.

But whatever she said, it must have been good for, after a few minutes, Mr Bones marched back.

"All right," he said, giving Mona a funny look. "We'll go down to the allotments. And the boy had better be there. Or else!"

Chapter 8
Incredible Things do Happen

Mona led the way, the long way round. She did it cleverly as if she <u>was</u> going fast but really going slowly, to give Charley time to get there before them.

First, she stumbled on purpose and pretended she'd hurt her leg and they should get a stretcher.

Next she insisted
that she and Fang
could hear a tiger
in a garden on
Da Gama Avenue and
they'd better all climb
trees to be on
the safe side.

Then, at the entrance to the allotments, there was a natural hold-up. The gates were locked and Mona's mother had to run back and borrow a key.

By the time they were actually marching along the allotment canal, Mona figured Charley had to be there.

And to her relief, as they rounded the last bend, there he was. Doing something so brilliant that for a split second it nearly confused her.

The Hairy Hands Headquarters

Knee-deep in cabbages, he was signing.
And signing BIG. In fact he was signing
so big he wasn't just using his hands. He
was using his arms and legs, his feet, his
head, his whole body. It was incredible.

"What's he doing?" growled Mr Bones.

"What do you THINK he's doing?"

Mona cried triumphantly. "He's talking
to the Hairy Hands of course! Because
though Hairy Hands can reach out and
take anyone anywhere, they can't talk
English, can they?"

"Bbbut ... what is he ...saying?"
breathed Lily's mother, spellbound.

"He's saying," said Mona, without even hesitating, "thanks for offering to take me on an adventure in far away lands, Hairy Hands, and be an explorer and ride on crocodiles and things, but I've got to get home or my dad will be cross which he already is because you crunched my bike and my mum will be home from work and start worrying …

"…and the Hairy Hands are saying back, 'sorry about your bike Charley. I'll try and reach in a bike shop and get you another one but you're mine now and the only thing that will make me give you back is–'."

Lily and Fang both had the same thought.

"Er ..." Mona was actually about to say 'if your dad agrees not to wallop you' but she didn't. She couldn't say another word. For now, something even more incredible than Charley's signing was happening.

Scowling–growling Mr Bones was no longer scowling and growling. He was laughing. He was roaring with laughter. He was snorting and laughing so much tears were squirting out of his eyes like water from a half-full water pistol.

"Never seen nothing like it in all my life!" he roared, clambering through the cabbages and slapping Charley on the back. "What you kids will get up to next, I'll never know. But for that performance, you old ragamuffin, son of a gun ..." he slapped Charley on the back again making him jump, "you deserve a medal, tell me I'm wrong or what!"

Chapter 9
A New Bike
And Almost The Whole Story

And the next day, when Charley-Knees came limping in to class, he couldn't wait to tell Mona what that medal was.

"A new bike!" he breathed. "Can you believe it? A whole new bike and nothing for wrecking the old one. Not even a ticking off!"

Just then Miss Gotto called the class to sit quietly on the rug for morning news.

"And looking at the state of Charley," she said, "I'd say he has something to share with us."

"Mona the Vampire," said Mona.

"Yeah … and with Lily …" stammered Charley.

"Lily the Second Vampire *and* Fang the Vampire Cat," said Mona.

"Yeah … and them …" said Charley. "Let Mona tell you … she knows better than me what happened … "

So Mona stood up and told the whole

story. Or rather she told almost the whole story and certainly the parts that made everyone go 'oooh' and 'aaah' and 'are there really such things as Hairy Hands?'.

What she didn't say was what her mother had said to Mr Bones to make him believe her, because she didn't know and her mother wouldn't tell her.

Most importantly, however, she did not say what she'd seen behind the old sofa in the Napps' front room.

And afterwards when she and Charley were feeding the fish, Charley said ...

"And if you ever want to ride my new bike," he said, "just say and you can."

"OK," said Mona. "I will."

"Only I can't teach you any stunts," said Charley, "not on my new bike, in case it gets wrecked."

"OK," said Mona. "I don't mind no stunts."

Then she skipped over to Miss Gotto's table.

"Tomorrow," she said, "I think the whole class should come as vampires because the Hairy Hands might still be about."

"Yes," said Lily, taking a finger out of her mouth. "They're not going back to China till Thursday."

Mona the Vampire
by Hiawyn Oram
Illustrated by Sonia Holleyman

Collect all the fangtastic *Mona the Vampire* stories!

☐ 1 **Mona the Vampire and the Hairy Hands**
ISBN 1 84121 859 6   £2.99

☐ 2 **Mona the Vampire and the Big Brown Bap Monster**
ISBN 1 84121 861 8   £2.99

☐ 3 **Mona the Vampire and the Tinned Poltergeist**
ISBN 1 84121 855 3   £2.99

☐ 4 **Mona the Vampire and the Jackpot Disaster**
ISBN 1 84121 857 X   £2.99

Look out for the novelty book,

☐ **Mona the Vampire's Diary by Sonia Holleyman**
ISBN 1 86039 8804   £8.99

Mona the Vampire books are available from all good bookshops,
or can be ordered direct from the publisher:
Orchard Books, PO BOX 29, Douglas IM99 1BQ
Credit card orders please telephone 01624 836000
or to fax 01624 837033
or e-mail: bookshop@enterprise.net for details.

To order please quote title, author and ISBN
and your full name and address.
Cheques and postal orders should be
made payable to 'Bookpost plc'.
Postage and packing is FREE within the UK
(overseas customers should add £1.00 per book).

Prices and availability are subject to change.